No Mush Today

by **Sally Derby**

illustrated by **Nicole Tadgell**

Lee & Low Books Inc. • New York

What Is Mush?

Mush is cornmeal that has been stirred into boiling water and cooked until it has turned into a thick, soft sort of porridge. Nonie eats hers out of a bowl, like oatmeal, with milk and sugar or syrup poured over it. Mush may also be chilled overnight in a loaf pan, then sliced thin and fried crisp in bacon drippings. Served with butter and maple syrup, fried mush is a hearty breakfast. Grits and polenta are also types of cornmeal similar to mush.

Text copyright © 2008 by Sally Derby
Illustrations copyright © 2008 by Nicole Tadgell
LEE & LOW BOOKS Inc., 95 Madison Avenue, New York, NY 10016
leeandlow.com

Manufactured in China
Book design by Mina Greenstein
Book production by The Kids at Our House
The text is set in ITC Stone Sans
The illustrations are rendered in watercolor
10 9 8 7 6 5 4 3 2 1
First Edition

Library of Congress Cataloging-in-Publication Data
Derby, Sally.
No mush today / by Sally Derby ; illustrated by Nicole Tadgell. — 1st ed.
    p. cm.
Summary: A young girl who is tired of eating mush for breakfast every day seeks solace with her grandmother, but comes to realize that she misses her family after all.
ISBN 978-1-60060-238-2
[1. Family life—Fiction. 2. Grandmothers—Fiction. 3. African Americans—Fiction.] I. Tadgell, Nicole, ill. II. Title.
PZ7.D4416No 2008
[E]—dc22   2007049037

To Steve and David, because family circles are expandable and love is limitless —S.D.

To Maggie, Sharaya, and Ducky —N.T.

"Not gonna eat my mush.
Not gonna eat it!" I say.

Squishy, yucky, yellow stuff—
mush is baby food.

Puttin' on my shiny shoes,
goin' over to Grandma's.

No mushy mush at Grandma's house.
No bawlin' baby there.

Grandma *attends* when I'm talkin',
calls me her Sweet Pea Nonie.

"Grandma, I'm comin' to live with you."
She hugs me and says, "I see!"

Off we go to grown-up church,
shiny shoes and Sunday hat.

"Mornin', Miss Charlotte," folks call out.
"How you doin', Nonie?"

Daddy winks when he passes the plate,
tryin' to make me smile.

I frown instead, drop my offerin' in—
ten pennies, a nickel, a dime.

Open church doors, laughin', huggin',
sunshine streamin' in.

Everyone's askin', "See you there?"
"See you at the picnic?"

Nobody told *me* 'bout a picnic today.
Nobody, nobody, no one.

"Come on, Sweet Pea," Grandma says.
"We'll all go together."

Church ladies' picnic is better than mush—
lemonade, chicken, three kinds of cake!

"How's your mama?" church ladies ask.
"How's that baby brother?"

Grandma's bones want a Sunday sit,
my bones want to move.

"Give you a boat ride?" Daddy asks.
Maybe, maybe . . . "All right," I say.

Daddy likes to show me things—
turtles, fishes, ducks.

"Ducklings stick with their families," he says.
"Lots to learn from ducks."

Next to paddleboats, I like swings.
Whooee! Watch me fly.

My swing is goin' way, way up
with Daddy pushin' me.

Grandma comes, says, "Time to go.
Bathtub's waitin', Nonie."

Families leavin' one by one,
goin' home together.

Momma's waitin' by the gate,
baby's reachin' for me.

"Look at him smilin'," Momma says.
"We're so glad you're home."

"Baby's been missin' me some?" I ask.
Momma nods, attendin' now.

Maybe I'll sleep home one more night.
Maybe . . . maybe . . . if . . .

"Promise, Momma,
promise, please.
PROMISE—
no mush tomorrow!"